Books by
Miriam Schlein

THE BEST PLACE
BIG LION, LITTLE LION
BILLY, THE LITTLEST ONE
HERE COMES NIGHT
SNOW TIME
THE WAY MOTHERS ARE

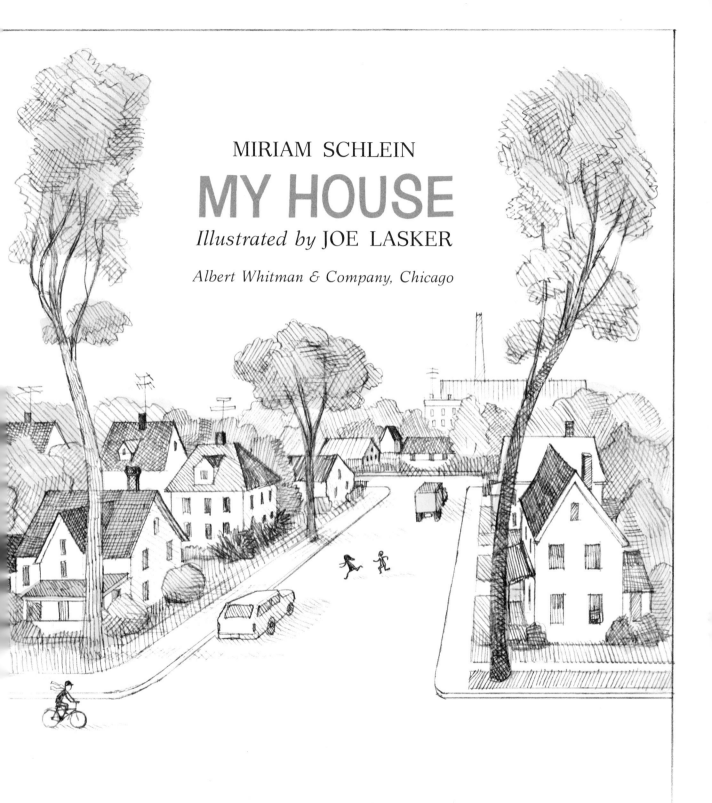

MIRIAM SCHLEIN

MY HOUSE

Illustrated by JOE LASKER

Albert Whitman & Company, Chicago

ISBN 0-8075-5357-3; L.C. Catalog Card 79-165820   Text ©1971 by Miriam Schlein; Illustrations ©1971 by Joe Lasker
Published simultaneously in Canada by George J. McLeod, Limited, Toronto Lithographed U.S.A. All rights reserved

There are lots of houses
around where I live.
One of them is MY HOUSE.
That's the most important
one—to me.

It is not the biggest house
or the newest house.

Some other houses have bigger trees
in front, and they have more
vegetables growing in their gardens.

But this one is MY HOUSE.

My house is where I come home,
when I have been away.

It is where my bed is,
and all my things,
and the people that I love best.

My house is where my books are,
my shells,

my little brother,
my father and mother.

My house was very much like
any other house before
we moved in.

But then we moved in.
And that's when it became special.

My father put up
shelves for *my* things.

We painted the closets
and hung our own clothes in them.

We painted the rooms
colors that *we* like.

We hung up pictures and
things that *we* like to
look at.

All these things helped make it *our* house.

It was spring when we moved in.

We planted grass seed,
and the grass grew.

It's nice to sit on.

There were lots of flowers
growing outside.

We weeded and watered them,
and cut some flowers,
and brought them into the house.

The flowers made things cheery,

made it smell nice.

When a house is your house
you get to know it
like a friend.

You understand things about it
that other people don't.

There is a scratching, growling noise
when the wind blows.

It's nothing scary.

"Oh," you say. "That is the
branch of the dogwood tree,
brushing against the window."

Whooo
    Whooo—

There is a whistling noise.

You know what that is, too.

"Oh," you say. "Someone has left
the chimney flue open.

That is just the wind
blowing through it."

A house grows with you.

It grows older with you,
and sometimes it grows bigger.

Sometimes your family gets bigger,
and you need more rooms in the house.

So they are added on.

A house has to be fixed up
and taken care of, too. Inside and out.

There is lots of work to do.

Sometimes I look at my house
and I think of all the things
that happened there.

The time I was sick.

The time Daddy fell down
and hurt his leg.

That time Mommy dropped
the spaghetti on the floor!

I think of all the times
my Daddy sat by that window
and read to me.

I think of all the cold mornings
I would stick just my feet
out from the covers,
and Mommy would put my socks on
for me—so I could stay warm
for a little bit longer.

My house is where very special
things happen to me.
Things that I remember.

My house is where my friends
can come to see me.

It is where people call me up.

It is where packages come in the
mail for me.

And when I have gone out,
no matter where I have been,
even though I have had the most
wonderful time, it is the place
I am always happy to come home to.

My House.

MIRIAM SCHLEIN has brought a special understanding to books for young children. She has chosen themes from everyday life, but presented them in a way that answers unspoken questions and offers the warmth of a shared experience. In *The Way Mothers Are,* for example, there is reassurance that a mother's love is not withdrawn when a child misbehaves, a fear children often feel but rarely express in words.

Although Miriam Schlein now lives in Westport, Connecticut, she was born and grew up in Brooklyn. She graduated from Brooklyn College and began a career in writing that by now has included adult fiction and more than forty books for children. She is a member of the Authors Guild.

JOE LASKER, like Miriam Schlein, grew up in Brooklyn. As a child he drew, read, and walked miles every day. Among his favorite books were those illustrated by N. C. Wyeth. He had his professional training at Cooper Union Art School in New York City and has won a number of coveted prizes for his painting. He is a member of the National Academy of Design and has exhibited in one-man shows in New York and Philadelphia.

Joe Lasker has illustrated three of Miriam Schlein's most popular books: *Snow Time; Big Lion, Little Lion,* and *The Way Mothers Are.* The draftsmanship, composition, and insights that distinguish Joe Lasker's easel painting give strength to his illustrations for children's books. There is, in addition, warmth and humor that communicate to the youngest child.